We Thought You Were a Platypus

Platypus Facts

A Mammal that hatches from an egg

About 2-5 lbs in weight

Male has venomous spines on his feet

Uses rocks and gravel to help chew its food

Can sense grubs and other food with its bill

Lives in riparian habitaits

Sleeps in a small burrow

This is a book about a baby named Charlie.

His parents didn't quite know what to expect...

One day, your mother said that she had a funny feeling in her tummy.

Her tummy felt very strange, she said,
like something was swimming inside it.

I'm not sure
what it is.

We decided to talk to the Doctor to see what was going on.

So we went to visit the Hospital.

Dr. Christina asked your mother a lot of questions and listened to her heart.

Then she poked around and looked at your mother's tummy with a special machine.

Yep, You are having a Baby!

Dr Christina said there was a baby in her tummy and we could even see it on the machine!

WAIT A MINUTE!!!!

"That is a Platypus!" I told your mother, with excitement!

Dr. Christina was right. There was a baby in your mother's tummy.

A BABY PLATYPUS!

It was quite apparent to your mother and me that an adorable baby platypus was growing inside of her.

We raced home to research how to care
for our baby Platypus.

They like to play at night.
They are nocturnal!
They like to eat grubs
and freshwater shrimp!
The Happy Platypus
Grubs! Yum!

We began digging a river habitat for our Platypus in which to play.

We filled it with grubs and muck.

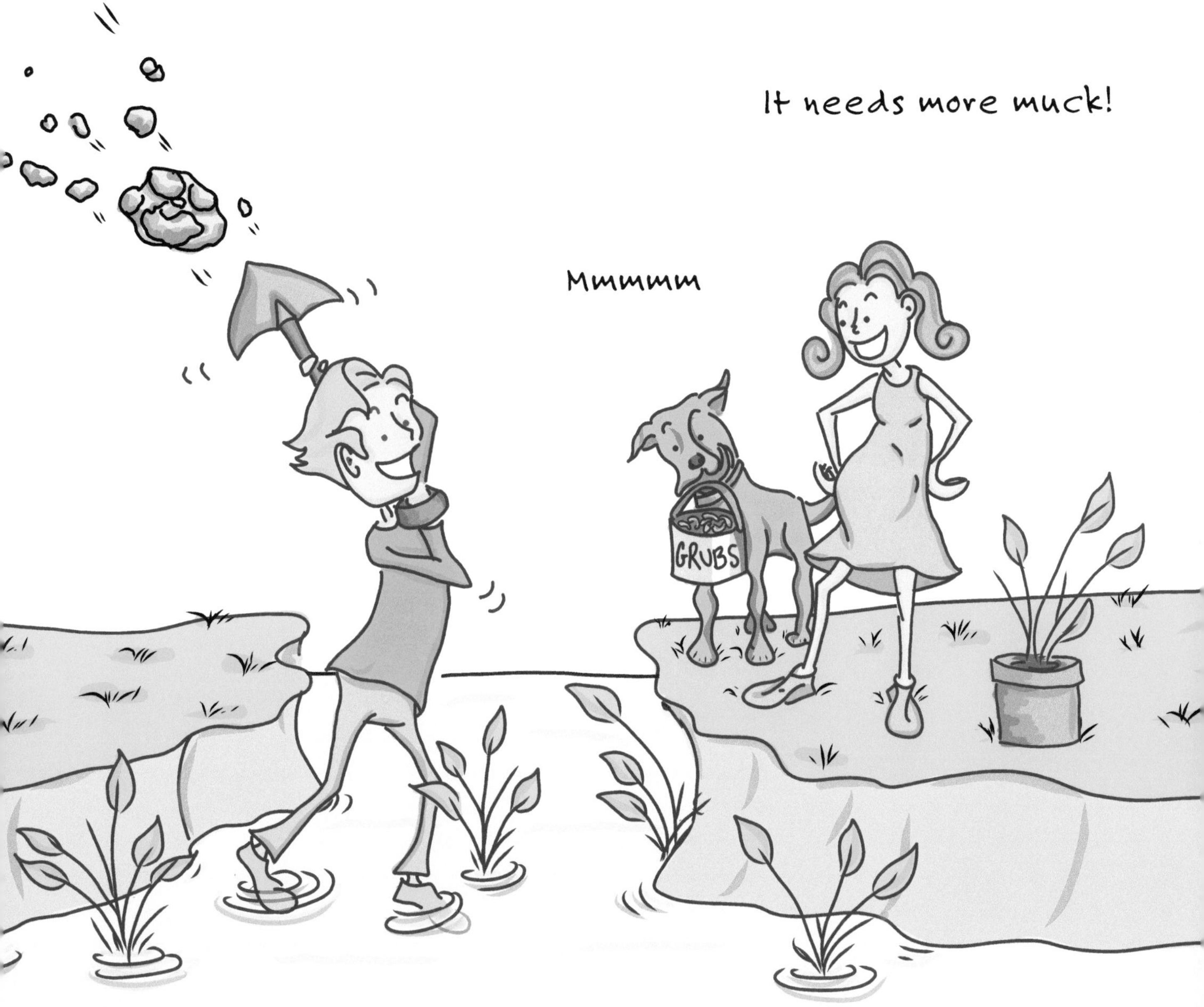
It needs more muck!
Mmmmm
GRUBS

Your mother and I were very excited and watched our Platypus get bigger in her tummy!

When our Platypus got very big, we went back to Dr. Christina...

Just then, your mother squeezed her eyes shut, wiggled her tummy and...

To our delight, YOU came out! And you weren't a platypus at all!

It's a baby Boy!!!!!

We took you home and loved you ever after.

And we gave the river to the dog.

The End

Baby Facts

Also a mammal, but doesn't hatch

Twice the size of a platypus

Does not have venomous spines

Should avoid chewing on rocks and gravel

Can sense when it's time for a snuggle

Lives in a house

Sleeps in a crib

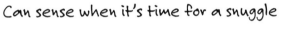
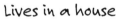

Special thanks to Charlie Aster for letting us bring him into the world, Jo Piazza for being his mother and Karen Oppenheimer and Pete Petitt for inspiration.

CPSIA information can be obtained
at www.ICGtesting.com
Printed in the USA
LVHW072252070219
606851LV00007B/14/P

9 780368 061448